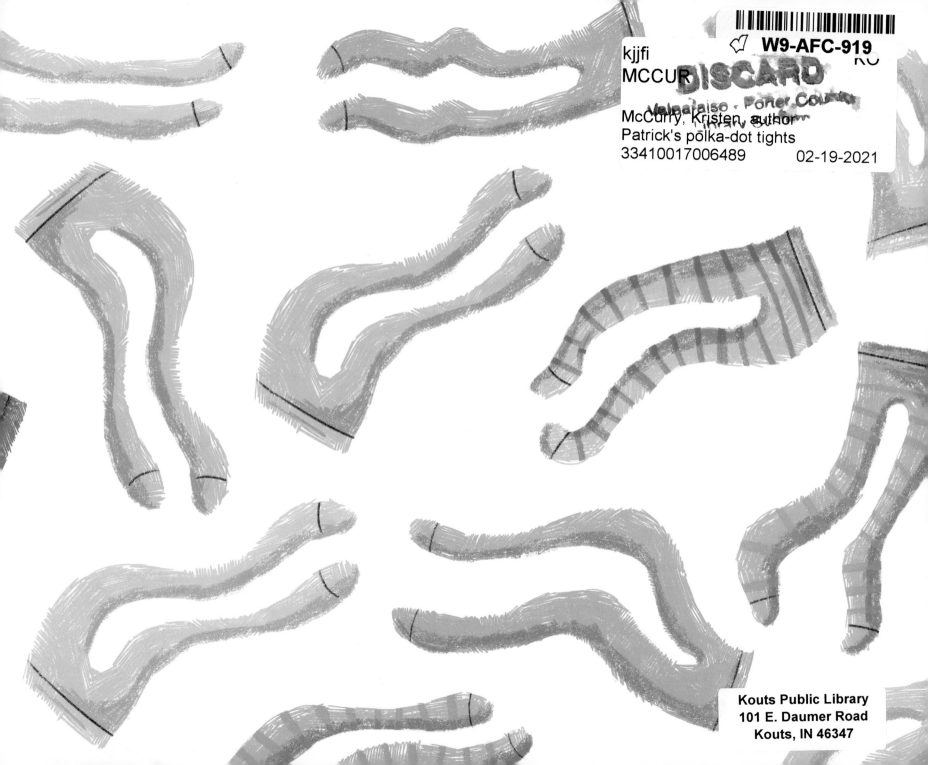

PATRICK'S POLKA-DOT TIGHTS

written by Kristen McCurry   illustrated by MacKenzie Haley

CAPSTONE EDITIONS
a capstone imprint

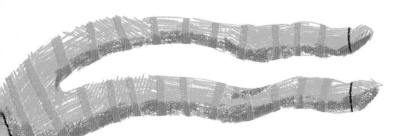

Patrick's Polka-Dot Tights is published by
Capstone Editions, an imprint of Capstone.
1710 Roe Crest Drive
North Mankato, Minnesota 56003
www.capstonepub.com

Library of Congress Cataloging-in-Publication Data
is available on the Library of Congress website.

ISBN: 978-1-68446-069-4 (hardcover)
ISBN: 978-1-68446-070-0 (ebook PDF)

Summary: Patrick loves to play with his sister's tights. There are so many things
he can do with them! When Penelope takes the tights back and ruins them,
Patrick is devastated. Is there anything that will make Patrick feel better?

Designer: Bobbie Nuytten

Printed and bound in China. PO3741

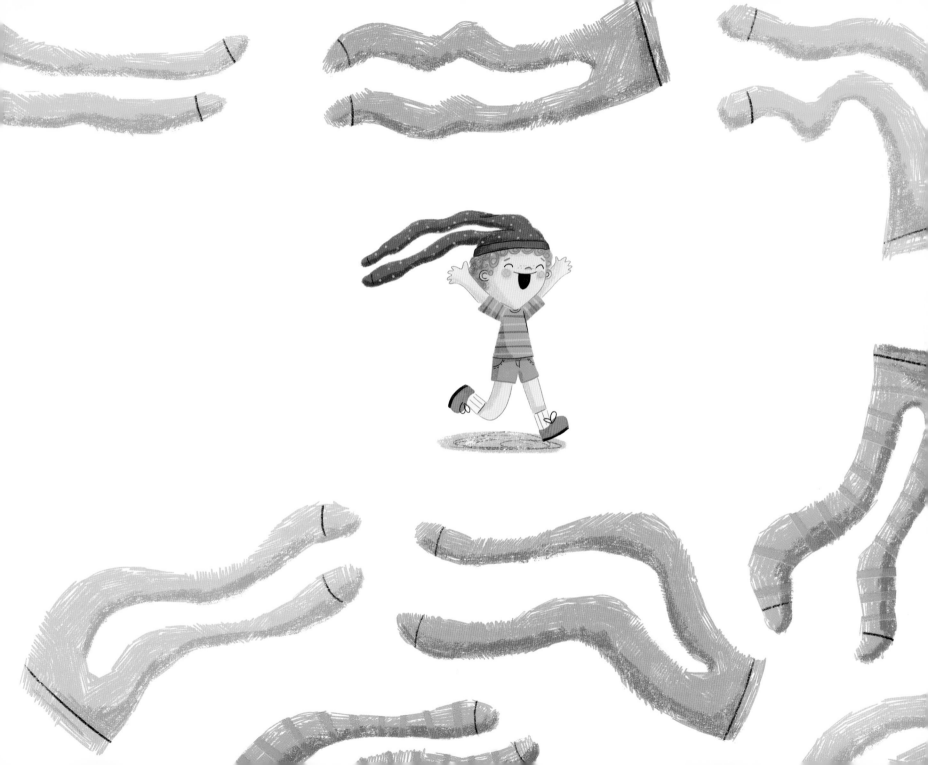

Patrick's tights were perfect and purple and had tiny
polka dots that stretched into ovals when he pulled them.

He liked to wear them under his snow pants
because they weren't too bulky.

He liked to wear them when he played dress up
and went to have tea with the queen of Tentsylvania.

He liked to wear them to bed because
they kept chilly air from tickling his toes.

But Patrick's purple polka-dot tights
were not *his* purple polka-dot tights.

They were his sister Penelope's,
and Penelope didn't care about the
tights . . . most of the time.

"Mom!
Patrick took my tights again!"

Penelope screamed as she was trying to get ready for another piano recital, which was the ONLY time she ever wore her tights.

It wasn't fair. Patrick wanted those purple polka-dot tights for himself. Penelope didn't deserve those tights. She failed to appreciate their many uses.

Like rescuing bears from drowning at sea . . .

. . . or taking your hot dog for a walk.

The tights were perfect as a
bandana that flows in the wind on
a great motorcycle adventure . . .

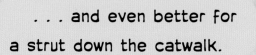

. . . and even better for
a strut down the catwalk.

After the recital, Patrick's family went out for ice cream.

Patrick picked strawberry with four cherries on top.

Penelope picked a hot fudge sundae with extra hot fudge.

Then disaster struck.

"Noooooooooo!"

Penelope had RUINED Patrick's
                              perfect
                                    purple
                                          polka-dot tights.

Patrick *knew* she didn't
deserve those tights. Patrick
sniffled in the car. He just
wanted to get home.

But instead of going home, Patrick's mom stopped at the superstore.

"Divide and conquer!" Patrick's mom said.

Patrick's dad and Penelope went to the light bulb section for light bulbs.

Patrick and his mother went to the toilet paper section for toilet paper . . .

to the laundry detergent section for laundry detergent . . .

and to the milk section for a gallon of milk.

The family all met up at the checkout. Penelope and Patrick's dad
appeared with the light bulbs . . . and a mysterious, colorful package.

"Here you go, buddy.
These are just for you."

Patrick loved his new
tights! They were great
for playing mummies . . .

. . . and for performances that required extra hair.

They zipped his sloth
through the rain forest . . .

. . . and provided endless entertainment at Grandpa's birthday party.

Patrick loved his new tights, but he kept the old purple polka-dot tights too. Because even with the sundae stain, Patrick's purple polka-dot tights were still perfect.

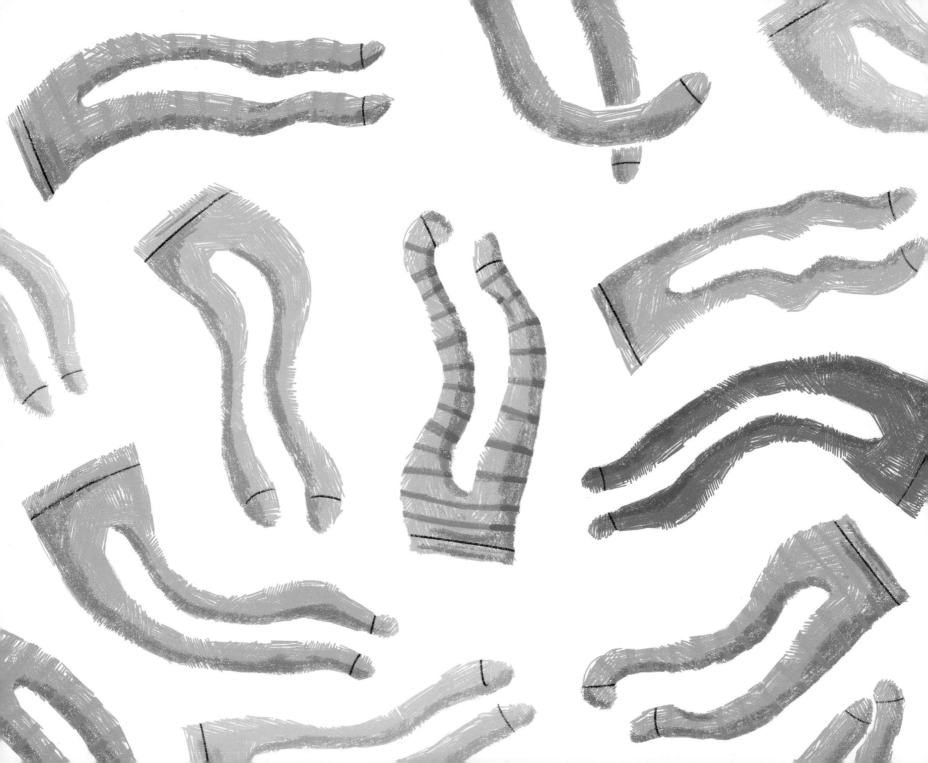